CLOUDLAND

Other books by John Burningham

A Red Fox Book

Published by Random House Children's Books
61-63 Uxbridge Road, London W5 5SA

A division of Random House UK Ltd
London Melbourne Sydney Auckland
Johannesburg and agencies throughout the world

Copyright © 1996 John Burningham

7 9 10 8 6

First published in Great Britain by
Jonathan Cape Ltd 1996
Red Fox edition 1999

Printed in Singapore

RANDOM HOUSE UK Limited Reg. No. 954009

ISBN 9780099711612

Cloudland

John Burningham

RED FOX

They had spent the day high up in the mountains.
So high were they that they could look at the
clouds below them.

"It's getting late and the light is fading fast,"
said Albert's father. "We must hurry down
before it gets dark."

...Then something terrible happened.
Albert tripped and fell off a cliff.

Albert's mother and father looked everywhere
but they couldn't find him. They were very sad
because they loved their little Albert.

Albert was lucky. The children who live in the clouds had seen him falling and said some magic words.

They either said,
"Fumble gralley goggle ho hee,"

or
"Teetum waggle bari se nee,"

or was it
"Gargle giggle fiddle num dee"?

Albert found himself becoming really light and the Cloud Children caught him.

"We'll make you a bed in the clouds, Albert," they said. "You must be tired after your fall."

When Albert woke up the next morning, the Cloud Children had made breakfast.

"After breakfast we're all going to climb up those tall clouds and play jumping games," they told him.

Albert really enjoyed jumping.
He wasn't at all afraid because he felt
light as a feather. After the jumping
games they played cloud ball – but
the clouds were becoming darker
and darker.

"There's going to be a thunderstorm.
Let's make as much noise as we can,"
said the children.

Then it began to rain.

"We're going for a swim now, Albert,"
said the Cloud Children.

After the rain came a beautiful rainbow
and they all painted pictures until it was
time to go to bed.

The next day there was a strong wind
and they were able to have races.

They raced each other on little clouds
which was great fun until Albert found
he was being left far behind.

Albert was all on his own.

The other children were drifting further
and further away.

Suddenly, there was a terrific noise
and a rush of air, and Albert was nearly
knocked off his cloud.

But the plane left a perfect path for Albert
and he was able to walk to the other children.

Albert was really enjoying his time in the clouds and the games with the children but one night, as he looked down from his cloud bed, he saw the lights of a city below and he thought of his mother and father and his own little bed.

"I WANT TO GO HOME," he said.

He said it so loudly it reached the ears of the Queen.

"Now what's all this about," she said. "Nobody has ever asked to go home from the clouds before."

"I want to be with my mother and father again," said Albert.

The Queen felt sorry for Albert and she thought for a long time.

At last she said, "I have a plan. It will be difficult but I'll try to make our clouds drift over where you live."

So while Albert and the Cloud Children spent their days playing and, each night, Albert slept in his cloud bed, the Queen got in touch with the wind.

Until one day she said,

"Albert, tomorrow we'll be over your home. But first we're going to give a party for you and I've invited the Man in the Moon."

Next evening, the clouds drifted over the city where Albert lived. The Queen and the Cloud Children shook hands with Albert and said goodbye.

Then the Queen said the magic words backwards. She either said,

"Hee ho goggle gralley fumble,"

or *"Nee se bari waggle teetum,"*

or was it *"Dee num fiddle giggle gargle"*?

The next thing Albert remembered
was that he was back in his own
little bed in his own room and his
mother and father were with him.

Albert sometimes wishes he could
be back playing with the Cloud
Children and he tries to remember
the magic words.

People hear Albert saying strange things to
himself – things like *"Nari blooy beany hoo,"*
or *"Meeky magi diddle hee doh,"*
but he can never get it quite right.

"There goes Albert talking to himself,"
they say. "He always did have his head in
the clouds."